This book belongs to

....

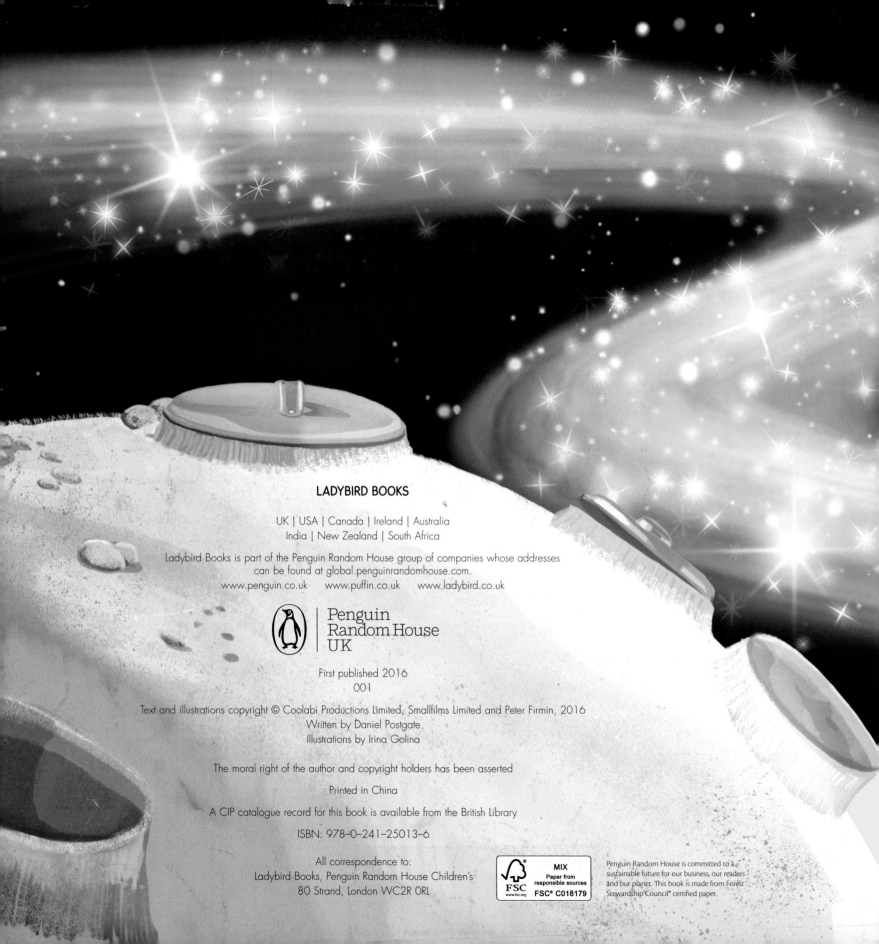

LADYBIRD BOOKS

UK | USA | Canada | Ireland | Australia
India | New Zealand | South Africa

Ladybird Books is part of the Penguin Random House group of companies whose addresses
can be found at global.penguinrandomhouse.com.
www.penguin.co.uk   www.puffin.co.uk   www.ladybird.co.uk

Penguin
Random House
UK

First published 2016
001

Printed in China

A CIP catalogue record for this book is available from the British Library

ISBN: 978-0-241-25013-6

All correspondence to:
Ladybird Books, Penguin Random House Children's
80 Strand, London WC2R 0RL

Clangers

SMALL'S BIRTHDAY TREAT

DANIEL POSTGATE

Today is Small Clanger's birthday.

But no one seems to
be around to celebrate.

Ah! That's because they're busy making presents. Granny is knitting something special . . .

Tiny is picking flowers
in the garden . . .

The Soup Dragon and her baby
are choosing secret treasures
from the deeper caves . . .

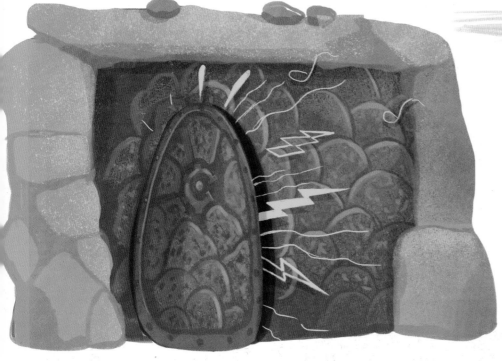

And Mother and Major
are making things in
the workshop.

Even the Iron Chicken is busy.
She's trying to find a present for
Small from all the junk in her nest.

But Small still thinks there is no one around.
"I suppose I might as well go back to bed!" says Small.

Soon Small is fast asleep, and he dreams about his birthday presents.

What he'd really like is a
scooter, just like Tiny has.

At last everyone is ready, and
they call to Small to come outside.

What a lot of lovely presents!

There's a birthday chair from Tiny, specially decorated with flowers.

There's a knitted hat from Granny, to keep Small warm while he's out fishing.

There's even glow-honey from the Glow-Buzzers. "How delicious and bright!" says Small.

The Soup Dragon and her baby have made a basket of treasures, collected from lots of different caves. Small likes the funny air fruit best!

Hello! Here comes the Iron Chicken,
flapping down with a heavy net
hanging from her beak.

It's full of her favourite junk.
She couldn't decide what to give
to Small, so she's brought it all.

"Thank you for my wonderful presents," Small says.

"Oh! We almost forgot," says Major.
"Here's our present," Mother says with a smile.

Small rushes to open it.

It's a box of tools, with spanners and hammers and screwdrivers and everything.

"Oh," says Small. "Thank you.
Although I rather wanted a scooter."
"Ah," says Major. "Well, maybe
you can have a scooter next year."

"Stay and enjoy your presents now," says Mother.
"We're going to make you a delicious birthday cake."

And off they all go.

Small looks at his hat and his glow-honey and his air fruit and his chair and his space junk. They're not the scooter he had wanted, but they're very nice presents all the same.

Then Small looks at his box of tools. And he has an idea.

A very good idea!

A little later, everyone returns
with Small's birthday cake.

But where is Small?
He's nowhere to be seen.

"Look!" says Tiny.

"There he is!"

He's made something special
from all his new presents . . .

A SUPER SCOOTER!

"Hooray for Small!"
cry the Clangers and their
friends. "What a very
CLEVER Clanger he is!"

And it's a **wonderful** sight to see.
A real birthday treat for everyone!

It just goes to show the amazing things that
can be invented with a little bit of imagination.

The End